The Ladybird Christmas Book

Ladybird Books

The First Christmas

In the little town of Nazareth there lived a girl called Mary.

When she was old enough to marry, a carpenter named Joseph asked her to be his wife.

Mary was happy, because she loved Joseph. Soon she was busy getting everything ready for the wedding.

But God knew that Mary was as good as she was beautiful. He decided to ask her to do something special for him. He sent his angel, Gabriel, to visit Mary in Nazareth.

"God loves you and wants your help," Gabriel told her.

At first, Mary was frightened. But Gabriel said, "Don't be afraid. God wants you to be the mother of his child, his son. When the baby is born you must call him Jesus."

Now the name Jesus means *God is with us.*

Mary thought for a moment. Then she said, "I want to do whatever God wishes, so I agree."

In a dream, Gabriel also appeared to Joseph and told him about God's plan. He asked Joseph to help Mary.

Together, Mary and Joseph prepared for the birth of God's child.

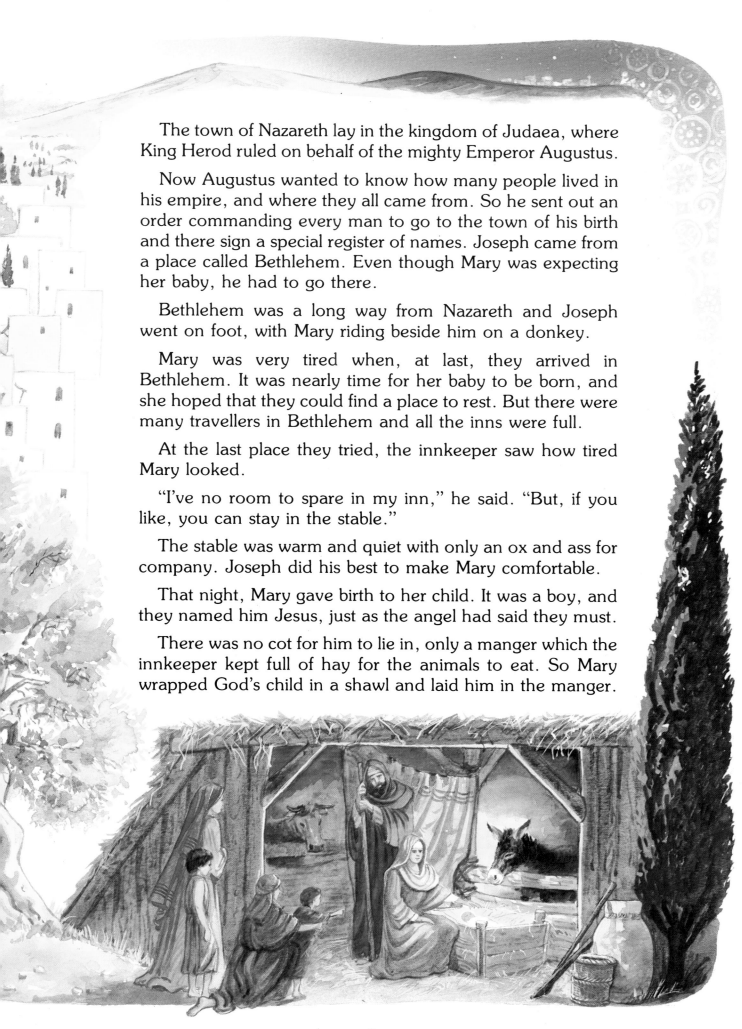

The town of Nazareth lay in the kingdom of Judaea, where King Herod ruled on behalf of the mighty Emperor Augustus.

Now Augustus wanted to know how many people lived in his empire, and where they all came from. So he sent out an order commanding every man to go to the town of his birth and there sign a special register of names. Joseph came from a place called Bethlehem. Even though Mary was expecting her baby, he had to go there.

Bethlehem was a long way from Nazareth and Joseph went on foot, with Mary riding beside him on a donkey.

Mary was very tired when, at last, they arrived in Bethlehem. It was nearly time for her baby to be born, and she hoped that they could find a place to rest. But there were many travellers in Bethlehem and all the inns were full.

At the last place they tried, the innkeeper saw how tired Mary looked.

"I've no room to spare in my inn," he said. "But, if you like, you can stay in the stable."

The stable was warm and quiet with only an ox and ass for company. Joseph did his best to make Mary comfortable.

That night, Mary gave birth to her child. It was a boy, and they named him Jesus, just as the angel had said they must.

There was no cot for him to lie in, only a manger which the innkeeper kept full of hay for the animals to eat. So Mary wrapped God's child in a shawl and laid him in the manger.

In the fields outside Bethlehem, some shepherds were keeping watch over their flocks. As they sat by their fire, an angel appeared to them. The fields shone with the light of God and the shepherds were terrified.

"Don't be afraid," said the angel. "I have great news for you, which you must share with everyone. Your saviour has been born in Bethlehem. You will find him wrapped in a shawl, lying in a manger."

Suddenly the sky was filled with light, and a great choir of angels began to sing,
Glory be to God in heaven!
And peace to all who are God's friends!

The shepherds hurried to Bethlehem and searched until they found the newborn baby. They told Mary and Joseph what the angels had said, and Mary listened in wonder, treasuring the shepherds' words.

Far away, in a land towards the east, three wise men saw a bright new star rise in the night sky. Because of their great learning they knew that it was the star of a newborn king.

4

The star began to move across the sky, and the wise men decided to follow it in the hope that it would lead them to the baby king.

After a long and difficult journey, the wise men eventually arrived in Bethlehem, where the star came to rest over the place where Jesus lay.

The wise men were full of joy as they hurried in to see Jesus. They had each brought a gift for the newborn king.

One had brought gold because that was the sign of a king, and Jesus was the king of heaven.

One had brought sweet-smelling frankincense because that was the sign of God's presence, and Jesus was God's son.

One had brought bitter myrrh because that was the sign of suffering, and Jesus would suffer and die on the cross when he became a man.

When they saw the baby king lying in his mother's arms the wise men fell to their knees and worshipped him. Then they set off on the long journey back to their own country.

When we celebrate Christmas today, we are remembering all the things that happened that first Christmas.

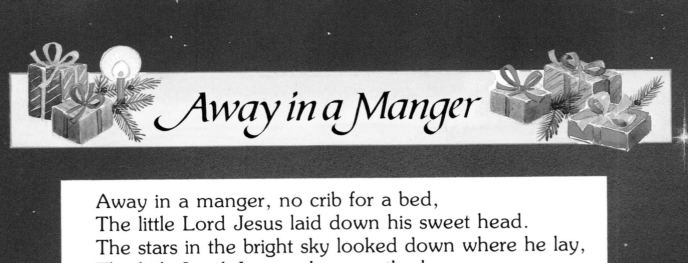

Away in a Manger

Away in a manger, no crib for a bed,
The little Lord Jesus laid down his sweet head.
The stars in the bright sky looked down where he lay,
The little Lord Jesus asleep on the hay.

The cattle are lowing, the baby awakes,
But little Lord Jesus, no crying he makes.
I love thee, Lord Jesus! Look down from the sky,
And stay by my side till morning is nigh.

Be near me, Lord Jesus; I ask thee to stay
Close by me for ever, and love me, I pray.
Bless all the dear children in thy tender care,
And fit us for heaven, to live with thee there.

THE GIFT BRINGERS

All over the world, traditional gift bringers visit children at Christmas and leave them presents as a reward for being good. The best known gift bringer is Santa Claus. His name comes from *Sinterklaas*, which is the Dutch name for St Nicholas. St Nicholas was the Bishop of Myra, in Asia. He was a rich man who used his wealth to help others. Although his feast day is on 6th December, he became so famous for his generosity that his name is now linked with Christmas.

St Nicholas was very popular in the Netherlands, and when Dutch people went to live in America they took their love of Sinterklaas with them. Soon, other Americans wanted to share Sinterklaas, and they gave him the new name of Santa Claus.

In Germany, the gift bringer is Christkindl, the Christ child. On Christmas Eve, children are not allowed into the room where the Christmas tree stands. When at last they are allowed in, they are always *just* too late to catch sight of Christkindl. But under the tree there are presents to prove that he was there.

Italian children receive their presents on 6th January. Their gift bringer is an old lady called Befana. Her sad story is told on the following pages.

Befana

One very cold winter's evening, the Widow Befana decided to go to bed early. She had been baking all afternoon, and she was tired.

She started to damp down the fire, when to her astonishment her little house began to fill with light. Befana rushed to the window and peered up into the sky, but all she could see was a thin moon and a handful of stars. The light that filled her home seemed to be coming from the fields nearby.

At first she thought that the shepherds had lit a bonfire to keep warm. But the light was pure and clear and steady, not at all like a bonfire. "Radiant!" thought Befana. "That's the word for it. Radiant."

And then the air was filled with singing. But such glorious singing, the like of which she had never before heard! "It's like the light," Befana muttered. "The music is radiant."

She wrapped herself up in a warm woollen cloak and ran outside, determined to find out what was going on. Down the path she sped, but the singing and the light faded into thin air before she reached the lane. She stood there for a moment, wondering what to do.

Then, from the direction of the fields, half a dozen shepherds came running towards her. One of them stopped for a moment to speak to her.

"We've seen angels!" he gasped. "They gave us a message! Our saviour has been born in Bethlehem! He's lying in a manger, wrapped in shawls!" The shepherd set off again after his companions, running for all he was worth, and Befana set out after him.

Then she remembered her fire. She didn't want it to burn out, for her house would soon get cold. So she went back and piled great pieces of turf on the fire to damp it down.

She set off again, but this time she got no further than the path when she was struck by a sudden thought. She ought to take this very important baby a birthday present!

Back to the house she trotted, racking her brains to think of a suitable birthday gift. The best she had to offer was a batch of the cakes she had baked that afternoon. Unfortunately they had got a little burned, and she didn't want to offer her saviour burned cakes. What would the neighbours say?

She decided to put off paying her respects until the following day. She went to bed, her mind filled with all the wonderful baking she would do next morning. Tomorrow she would bake some cakes that were worthy of a saviour!

But it took many days before Befana was at last satisfied with her work. How proud she was of the dozen cakes that she had cooked! All were perfectly golden and filled with nuts and fruit. The baby wouldn't be able to eat them, of course, but everyone else would be very impressed by her baking skills.

Befana walked into Bethlehem and asked directions to the baby's stable. But everyone she spoke to just shook their heads sadly. When at last she pushed the stable door open, Befana understood why. The place was empty except for an ox, munching on its hay and looking across at her with mournful eyes.

Then Befana began to weep. Her silly pride had made her miss the newborn saviour. "You fool!" she said, as the sobs racked her body. "What did he want with cakes? You should have given him your heart."

On the way home, Befana heard some rumours. The baby's parents had taken him to Egypt.

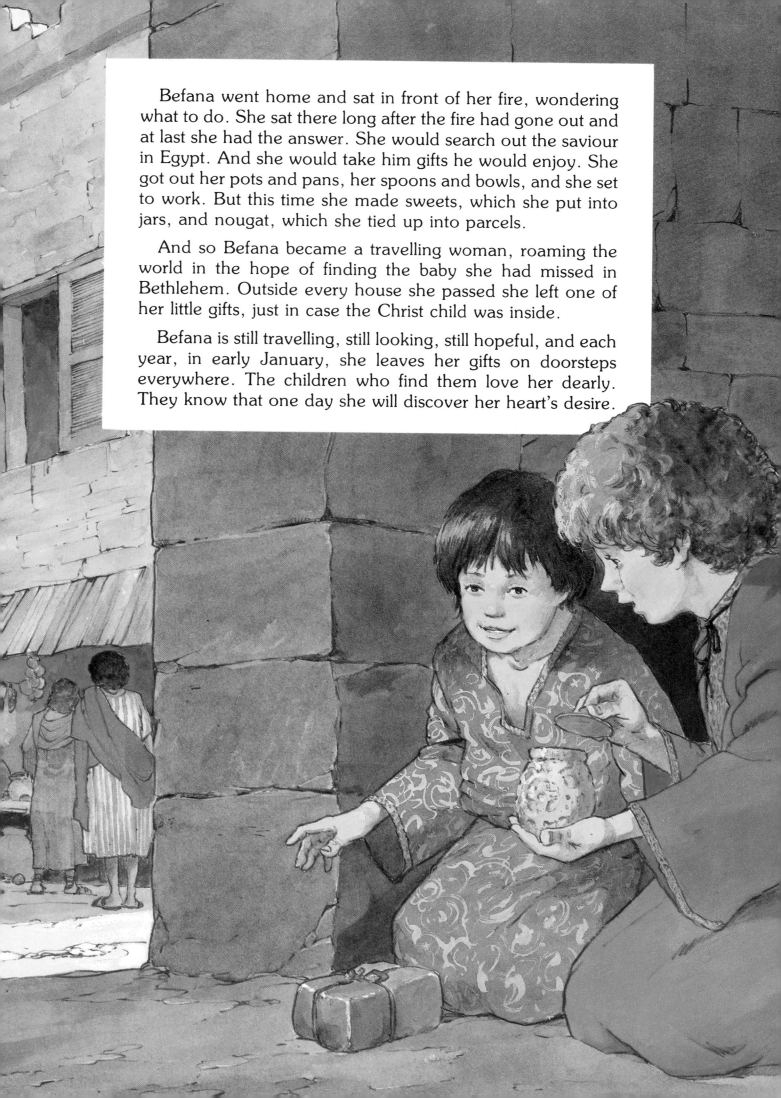

Befana went home and sat in front of her fire, wondering what to do. She sat there long after the fire had gone out and at last she had the answer. She would search out the saviour in Egypt. And she would take him gifts he would enjoy. She got out her pots and pans, her spoons and bowls, and she set to work. But this time she made sweets, which she put into jars, and nougat, which she tied up into parcels.

And so Befana became a travelling woman, roaming the world in the hope of finding the baby she had missed in Bethlehem. Outside every house she passed she left one of her little gifts, just in case the Christ child was inside.

Befana is still travelling, still looking, still hopeful, and each year, in early January, she leaves her gifts on doorsteps everywhere. The children who find them love her dearly. They know that one day she will discover her heart's desire.

The Gift of the Magi

Della and Jim were very young, and very poor, and they loved each other very much. Their tiny, threadbare flat was in a rundown part of New York City, but it had been their home since they were first married, and they were happy in it.

Now it was the day before Christmas, and Della was adding up her savings. One dollar and eighty-seven cents — that was all it came to. Just $1.87. And the next day would be Christmas.

Della flung herself onto the sofa and wept.

Only $1.87 to buy a present for Jim. She had spent so many happy hours thinking about what she would get him. It had to be something fine and precious, just like Jim himself. But what could she do with $1.87?

Suddenly Della stopped crying and sat up. She had an idea — why hadn't she thought of it before? Quickly she went to the mirror and pulled the pins from her hair.

Now, there were two possessions in which Jim and Della both took great pride. One was Jim's gold watch that had been his father's and grandfather's. The other was Della's beautiful brown hair, which now fell rippling and shining about her shoulders.

With trembling hands, Della did up her hair again. On went her old brown jacket and hat. With a whirl of skirts, she hurried downstairs to the street.

She walked until she came to a sign that read: "Madame Sofronie. Hair Goods of All Kinds". Della knocked on the door, and a woman answered.

"Will you buy my hair?" Della asked.

"Take off your hat and let's have a look at it," Madame said.

Down rippled the beautiful brown hair.

"Twenty dollars," said Madame.

"Okay. Do it quick," said Della. And Madame did. A few snips and she was finished.

For the next two hours, Della searched the shops for Jim's present. She found it at last, the one present that surely had been made for him and no one else: an elegant platinum watchchain. Grand as Jim's watch was, Della knew that he was ashamed of its shabby strap. With the platinum chain, he could consult his watch with pride in the finest company.

As soon as she got home, Della looked at her hair in the mirror. "If Jim doesn't kill me," she said to herself, "he'll say I look like the newsboy. But what could I do with a dollar and eighty-seven cents?"

At seven o'clock, holding the watchchain tightly in her hand, Della sat down to wait for Jim. When she heard his footsteps on the stairs, she said a silent prayer: "Please let him think I am still pretty."

The door opened and Jim walked in. He stared at Della with an expression she could not understand.

"Jim, darling," she cried, jumping up to hug him, "don't look at me that way. I had my hair cut off and sold it so I could buy you a Christmas present. It'll grow back — my hair grows awfully fast. Please, Jim, say 'Merry Christmas' and let's be happy. Wait till you see the gift I've got you!"

"You've cut off your hair?" said Jim slowly, as if he couldn't believe what he was seeing.

"Cut it off and sold it," said Della. "Don't you like me just the same? I'm still me, even without my hair."

Suddenly Jim seemed to wake from his trance. He took Della in his arms. Then he took a package from his pocket.

"Don't worry, Dell," he said. "No haircut could make me love you any less. But unwrap this package, and you'll see why I looked so disappointed."

Excitedly, Della tore off the paper. She gave a joyful cry, which instantly turned to tearful wailing.

For inside the package lay the set of combs Della had seen in a shop window on Broadway and longed for ever since. Beautiful tortoiseshell combs, with jewelled rims. They were expensive, she knew, and she had longed for them without the least hope of ever owning them. Now they were hers — and the beautiful hair they should have adorned was gone.

But she hugged the combs and tried to smile. Looking up with damp eyes, she said, "My hair grows so fast, Jim!"

Then she leapt up and cried, "Oh, oh! You haven't seen your present yet!" She held it out to him eagerly.

"Isn't it wonderful, Jim?" she said breathlessly. "I hunted all over town for it. You'll have to check the time a hundred times a day now. Give me your watch. I want to see how it looks."

But Jim just flopped down onto the sofa and smiled sadly. "Dell," he said, "let's put our Christmas presents away for now. They're too nice to use just yet." Then, taking a deep breath, he said, "I sold the watch to get the money for your combs."

The Magi, as you know, were the wise men who brought gifts to the baby Jesus. They were the first people ever to give Christmas presents, and because they were wise they chose their presents wisely. I have just told you the story of two young people who foolishly gave up their greatest treasures so they could give gifts to each other. But were they really foolish? I think not. People who give as they did, without thinking of themselves, are the wisest givers of all. They are the Magi.

Worried Arthur

Arthur was a penguin. And a worrier. Arthur worried about whether he would grow as tall as his father.

He worried because his hair stood on end. And now, of all things, Arthur was worried about Christmas!

One day Arthur came home from school. He looked even more worried than usual.

"And what have you been doing today?" asked Dad.

"Map of the world," mumbled Arthur. He didn't sound too happy about it.

"And where do *we* live?" asked Dad. He did hope Arthur had been concentrating.

"It's called Antarctica," said Arthur. "And it's near the South Pole."

"Well done, Arthur!" beamed Dad.

That night Arthur padded across the landing. He climbed onto Dad's bed and tugged at his pyjamas.

"I'm worried, Dad," he whispered.

Dad stopped snoring and woke up with a start. "What is it, Arthur?"

"It's the map of the world, Dad. We live at the SOUTH Pole and Santa Claus lives at the NORTH Pole. What if he gets tired before he gets here? What if he runs out of toys?"

"Well, you can stop worrying about THAT," said Dad firmly. "Santa Claus got down here all right when I was a lad. And he still had plenty of toys left!"

Arthur looked less worried. He trotted back to bed and fell asleep.

On the last day of term, Arthur brought home his school report. He hovered nervously while Dad read all about him.

"Well done, Arthur. You've worked hard all term. And, although your writing is rather illegible, it's nothing to worry about."

That night Arthur kept his light on late. It took him a long time to find 'illegible' in his dictionary. And, when he did, it was all very worrying.

In the middle of the night Arthur padded across the landing. He shuffled round the end of Dad's bed, and biffed him on the beak.

"I'm worried, Dad," he whispered.

Dad stopped snoring and woke up with a start. "What is it, Arthur?"

"It's my writing, Dad. What if Santa Claus can't read it? What if he doesn't bring the things on my list?"

"Well, you can stop worrying about THAT," said Dad firmly. "For your information, Santa Claus is the world's leading expert on handwriting. Good heavens, he'd soon be out of a job if he couldn't read double dutch."

Arthur looked less worried, and went back to sleep.

Two days before Christmas it began to snow heavily. Dad got out Arthur's toboggan. Then they made a snowman together. Arthur was tired out when he went to bed. But he still woke up worrying.

Just after midnight Arthur padded across the landing. He opened Dad's curtains.

"I'm worried, Dad," he whispered.

Dad stopped snoring and woke up with a start. "Whatever is it THIS time, Arthur?"

Arthur pulled Dad over to the window. "It's the weather, Dad. It's started to snow again. What if there's great big drifts on Christmas Eve? What if Santa can't get through?"

"Well, you can stop worrying about THAT," said Dad firmly. "You don't think Santa Claus will be put off by a bit of snow, do you? Whatever do you think he's got those hulking great reindeer for?"

Arthur looked less worried, and went back to sleep.

On Christmas Eve, Dad and Arthur decorated their tree. They put their presents underneath. And Arthur wrote his labels...very clearly. After supper Dad sat on the end of Arthur's bed and read him a story. It was Arthur's favourite, but he still looked worried.

"Now, look here, son," said Dad. "I could use a good night's sleep. So, if there's anything worrying you, you'd better get it off your chest."

"It's my room," whispered Arthur. "What if Santa Claus comes in my room and sees all my books and toys? What if he thinks I don't deserve any more?"

"Well, you can stop worrying about THAT," said Dad firmly. "If Santa Claus only brought presents to deserving children, he would only need to work part-time. But, if it makes you feel any better, we can leave him a note."

So Arthur and Dad left a message at the top of the stairs. It suggested – very tactfully – that Santa might like to leave Arthur's gifts on the landing.

As soon as they'd written the note, Arthur looked less worried.

"Now, there's just one more thing," said Dad.

"Yes, Dad?"

"If anything else worries you in the night, Arthur, KEEP IT TO YOURSELF till tomorrow!"

But that night Arthur and Dad both slept like logs. Next morning Arthur sat up in bed.

"OUCH!" He banged his head on the picture above his bed. "Yippee!" cried Arthur. "I must be growing."

He jumped out of bed and looked in the mirror. Arthur smoothed down his hair and...IT STAYED THERE! Then he looked out on the landing.

Sure enough, there was a stocking, filled with everything Arthur had asked for.

Arthur waited patiently for Dad to wake up. At last he came onto the landing.

"Merry Christmas, Arthur. And how are you feeling this morning?"

"I feel funny, Dad," said Arthur. Then he smiled. "It must be because...
I'M NOT WORRYING!"

19

Decorations

There's tinsel round the mirror
And a mobile by the door.
There's honesty and mistletoe,
We've not had THAT before.

There's snowspray on the windows,
Pearly patterns on the panes,
And right across the room runs
A mile of paper chains.

There's a snowman with a pipe
And a hat all made of felt,
And 'though he's snug and warm
I know he'll never melt.

There's holly and there's lollies
With the baubles on the tree.
And have you seen the lantern
I made when I was three?

There's Christmas cards and greetings
All threaded on a string,
And here's my special robin –
Be careful of his wing!

There's fairy lights and CANDLES –
A power cut would be great!
It won't be long till Christmas
And I can hardly wait.

Deck the Halls

Long before the birth of Christ, people decorated their homes with evergreens during the winter festivals. The evergreens, such as holly, ivy and mistletoe, kept their leaves all year round, and were a reminder that, despite the ice and snow, life would return to all plants when spring arrived.

Christians carried on using evergreens to decorate their homes to celebrate the birthday of Jesus. Holly was used because it is a symbol of good luck. Mistletoe is a symbol of love, and any girl who is kissed beneath a sprig of mistletoe will be sure of a happy marriage.

As more and more people went to live in towns and cities, it became increasingly difficult for them to get hold of evergreens at Christmas. So instead they used coloured paper which they cut and twisted into fancy shapes or streamers.

The most popular evergreen of all is the fir tree, or Christmas tree. The first person to have brought a fir tree indoors at Christmas is supposed to have been Martin Luther, a religious reformer who lived in Germany in the sixteenth century. He decorated the tree with candles to show his family how beautiful the stars had looked one night as he was walking through the forest.

Nowadays, Christmas trees are decorated with electric fairy lights, tinsel and shiny glass baubles, with an angel or star at the top. The star is to remind us of the star that led the three wise men to the stable in Bethlehem where Jesus was born.

The Magic Christmas Tree

Long ago, in a faraway land, there stood a beautiful fir tree. It was a special tree, for on its branches grew fairy lights and brightly coloured parcels. The lights always shone and the children could pluck a parcel by just reaching high into the branches.

And inside the parcels were the most wonderful presents! Tiny or large, each one was just what the children had always wished for! But they never took too many parcels, for they loved the magic tree. And so the tree flourished, and it seemed like Christmas every day of the year.

But one day a new little girl, called Sonja, arrived. When she saw the magic parcels, she wanted to take them all. With impatient hands she snatched down every parcel she could see. Soon the magic tree was quite bare.

How sad it looked! Without the magic parcels its branches began to droop. Then one by one the lights flickered and went out.

The children were upset and Sonja started to cry. She was now sorry for her impatience and greed.

"It's all my fault!" she cried. "Oh, what can I do to help?"

As she spoke, the last parcel, hidden out of sight near the top of the tree, floated gently down to the ground. Sadly the children unwrapped it. Then their eyes opened wide, for in the box lay a shining silver egg! It was still warm!

"Quick!" cried Olaf, the farmer's son. "We must find a hen to sit on the egg before it grows cold!"

Helga, the little hen, was delighted to help. She had never sat on a silver egg before. Perhaps it would hatch into a tiny silver chick? She clucked with excitement.

A week later the egg began to hatch. To the children's amazement, the shell cracked and out stepped a fairy just six inches tall! She was dressed in a white gown and on her head was a tiny silver crown. A wand sparkled in her right hand.

"Now," she asked the children in a soft, silvery voice, "what can I do for you?"

The children all spoke at once.

"The magic tree is not well," said Olaf sadly.

"And the lights have all gone out," said Ingrid, his little sister.

"And the parcels have stopped growing," said Henrik, Olaf's best friend.

The fairy listened thoughtfully.

"Well," she said at last. "All of you, not just Sonja, have been happy to *take* from the magic tree. You have never *given* it one thing in return! Why don't you give the tree some gifts for a change?"

The children were ashamed. They hurried home and opened their money boxes. Some bought little glass ornaments and hung these on the tree. Others bought tinsel and wound it in and out of the branches.

Still the tree drooped.

"It's not enough!" Sonja cried. "I shall give it my teddy bear!" It was her favourite toy and she was sad to part with it. But she fastened it firmly to the tree. The others followed. Olaf gave his colourful engine, Ingrid her prettiest doll. Soon the tree was covered with the children's favourite toys to thank it for *everything* it had given them.

The children waited. Suddenly, one of the lights glowed. Then one by one, they all lit up again! The branches picked up and tiny parcels appeared and grew bigger.

"Hurrah!" cried the children. "The magic Christmas tree is well again! The lights are bright, and the parcels are even prettier than before!"

"But what can we do to stop people from snatching all the parcels again?" asked Sonja, now smiling happily through her tears.

"I'll fly to the topmost branch!" said the fairy. "Whenever a parcel is snatched, I'll wave my magic wand. In the parcel, instead of a gift, there'll be an ugly stone!"

And so the tree grew strong, and once a year, when Christmas came, the children put ornaments and tinsel and other little gifts on its branches to say "thank you".

As for the fairy, she is still there at the top of the tree.

"Just in case!" she says with a smile.

A COMPUTER FOR SANTA CLAUS

Santa Claus looked round his office and sighed. There was paperwork everywhere, and it was still only November. Children were sending in their lists earlier than ever this year.

Santa cleared a space and sat down at his desk. But before he could start work, there was a loud knock at the door.

"It's a salesman," announced a reindeer. And in rushed a smart young man.

"Slick's the name," cried the salesman, "representing Greenland, Finland, Nomansland and the North Pole, on behalf of the Carefree Computer Company.

"Now, if I might be so bold," went on Mr Slick. He waved his arm at the mess. "You seem to be in urgent need of our services."

CLICK! Mr Slick's briefcase sprang open and out fell a pile of leaflets. Mr Slick grabbed the nearest.

"If I might suggest," he continued, "the Whizz Bang 2000 would seem to be ideal for this office. And what luck!" Mr Slick did his best to sound surprised. "If you purchase your Whizz Bang 2000 before December, you will receive an Utterly Essential computer program and a pack of reindeer games... ABSOLUTELY FREE!"

"PITTER PATTER, GUSH SPLATTER!"
Out streamed Mr Slick's sales talk. And, before
you could say 'Christmas Eve', Santa had signed
on the dotted line.

Ten days later a hefty package arrived.
The reindeer gathered round and beat their
hooves with excitement. When Santa opened
up the package, he found:
one Whizz Bang 2000 computer
one Utterly Essential computer program
one pack assorted reindeer games
one set of instructions
one plug and...
one note, which said:

> *Regret pressure of work prevents personal*
> *delivery and demonstration of computer.*
> *All your troubles are now behind you!*
>   *Signed...Nigel Slick*

"Humph!" said Santa. He started to read the instructions.
The reindeer hovered hopefully. But Santa was firm.

"There'll be no reindeer games today. I've got to sort out
these instructions."

It took Santa a long time to read the instructions. Every so
often he muttered, *'mumbo jumbo'* or *'new-fangled'* and
thumbed through his dictionary. But Santa's dictionary was
old and faded. The person who wrote it hadn't heard of
computers!

Santa decided to ring up Mr Slick, long-distance.

"Mr Slick is out, giving a demonstration," said the telephonist. She put Santa through to the Mumbo Jumbo Department.

The Mumbo Jumbo Department explained the meaning of the new-fangled words and Santa re-read his instructions.

By the time he had finished, his head was swimming. His eyes were smarting. Suddenly the workshop clock struck ten.

"Slithering sleighs!" cried Santa. "I'm off to bed."

Next morning Santa plugged in his Carefree computer.

CRASH! A group of reindeer skidded into the office.

"NOT YET!" said Santa, crossly. "There'll be no reindeer games until I've sorted out this Utterly Essential computer program."

Santa loaded his program into the machine and pressed a button on the keyboard.

"PING!" To Santa's surprise, the computer played a little jingle:

Carefree, Carefree, don't forget,
We're the best invented yet!

"Humph!" said Santa. "We'll see about that."

He pressed another button and read the words on the screen:

Carefree Computers bring you the
Utterly Essential program. Simply type
in name, age and location of each child.
List all the toys in your workshop and
the Whizz Bang 2000 will select the
ideal present for each child.

"Humph!" said Santa. "And just what do you think I'VE been doing for the last umpteen years?"

The computer had no answer to that. So it just played its silly jingle again.

"Oh, DO shut up!" snapped Santa.

It took all morning for Santa to type in the children's details. It took all afternoon to list out the toys. By the time he had finished, his back ached, his arms tingled and his legs were beginning to twitch!

What a day! "It's all yours!" he shouted to the reindeer. "I've had enough of computers."

PING ZING, ZING PING. The reindeer had a whale of a time with their games. It was all Santa could do to get them into bed by midnight. And then they didn't stay there. As soon as Santa was asleep, they crept back into his office and started playing games again. But then they began to squabble.

"It's MY go," cried the heaviest reindeer. He sat on the keyboard to prove his point.

CHATTER, CLUNK, CHATTER, went the computer. And then a terrible notice appeared on the screen.

You have just wiped out the computer's memory. Your free Utterly Essential program is now worthless. Please send to Headquarters for another. It will take an age and cost a bomb.

Your troubles have just begun!

The reindeer shot off to bed and hid their heads under the covers.

29

Next morning Santa yawned as he walked into the office. He still felt stiff all over. And he wasn't looking forward to his day's work at all. Santa sighed as he sat down in front of his Carefree computer. Then he read the message on the screen and smiled. Just at that moment the telephone began to ring.

It was Mr Slick, long-distance. Mr Slick's voice came and went because the line was bad.

"Urgent need of Whizz Bang 2000... special customer in Lapland... will buy back... name your price."

Santa re-read the notice on the computer screen and suddenly the line cleared. He gave his instructions to Slick, long-distance.

"Anything you say, Mr Claus," gabbled Slick gratefully. "I shall despatch the best ever selection of toys direct to the North Pole, forthwith if not sooner!"

Santa put down the receiver and stretched. All of a sudden he couldn't wait to start work. He closed his eyes and picked out a letter.

"Well, Nancy aged nine of Northampton, let's see what we can find for your list."

Santa whistled on his way to the workshop. He stopped to look in on the reindeer.

"Come on," he shouted cheerfully. "Get those heads from under the covers. There's a lot of catching up to do before Christmas!"

Christmas Eve at the Zoo

You'd never believe the hullabaloo –
It's Christmas Eve at the local zoo.
The hippos are wrapping,
The penguins are flapping,
"Have YOU got the string?"
Cries the kangaroo.

You'd never believe the terrible stew
Those chaps are in at the local zoo.
The jumbos are jumping,
The camels are grumping,
"Those horrible vultures
Have stolen the glue."

You'd never believe the type of to-do
That Christmas brings to the local zoo.
The lions are licking,
The tigers are sticking,
Oh, PLEASE help panda
– he hasn't a clue!

You'd never believe that the keeper's new
To watch him work at the local zoo.
He's cheering and chatting,
He's praising and patting,
"You're over-excited,
You Christmassy crew!"

You'd never believe it, can it be true?
They're fast asleep at the local zoo.
The parcels are ready,
The snoring is steady,
And here comes a sleigh
With...YOU KNOW WHO!

Wake Up, Webster, It's Christmas!

"Will Webster wake up in time for Christmas?" asked Tom.

"Now, I've explained all that," said Mum. "Tortoises need to sleep in the winter. Webster will wake up in the spring."

"But Webster will miss all the fun," said Tom. He pulled on his wellies and anorak, and trudged out to the garage.

Right at the back of the garage was a cardboard box. It was full to the brim with polystyrene shapes. And buried deep in the shapes was Webster.

Tom started to poke and prod.

"WAKE UP, WEBSTER!" he shouted. "IT'S NEARLY CHRISTMAS."

Mum caught Tom just in time.

"Leave Webster alone, Tom. Webster has hibernated and he is happy where he is."

The next day Tom went to school. In the morning the children sang carols and Tom played his recorder. During the afternoon they all made Christmas cards. Tom cut out a snowman, a gold bell and some holly. He glued them carefully onto the front of his card. Inside Tom wrote MERRY CHRISTMAS, WEBSTER and painted a picture of strawberries (strawberries were Webster's favourite food).

As soon as he got home, Tom rushed into the garage. He propped up Webster's card on the lawn mower and rummaged in his box.

Tom scooped out handfuls of polystyrene shapes and took a deep breath.

"WHILE SHEPHERDS WATCHED THEIR FLOCKS...!"

Tom played his recorder full blast into Webster's box. It was enough to wake a dinosaur!

Mum caught Tom just in time.

"Leave Webster alone!" she cried. "Webster will wake up when it's warm."

As soon as the holidays came, Tom went to play with his friend Ruth. They wrapped up warmly and set off for the park. Tom ran, Ruth skipped, Ruth's mum strode and Wilbur bounced. Wilbur was Ruth's dog and he was extremely frisky.

Suddenly Tom ran up to Ruth's mum. He took hold of her hand and looked up wistfully.

"Will Wilbur have fun at Christmas?" he whispered.

"You bet!" cried Ruth. "He'll sleep at the end of my bed on Christmas Eve. He'll help me open my stocking..."

"And, if he's a very good dog," whispered Ruth's mum, "he'll have some presents all of his own."

Tom was quiet when he got home. For the first time ever he asked to go to bed early.

But while Mum was watching TV, Tom crept downstairs again – and into the garage.

"UMPH!" Tom picked up Webster's box, and carried it carefully upstairs.

"WHOOPS!" Tom wobbled a bit, because the box was an awkward shape.

"PHEW!" Tom reached his bedroom and put Webster down – right by the radiator!

"Please wake up, Webster. There's only a few days left."

Mum caught Tom just in time.

"There are polystyrene shapes all over the stairs," she cried. "And WHATEVER are you doing with Webster?"

"Warming him up for Christmas," said Tom in a small voice.

Mum took the box back to the garage. She swept up the polystyrene shapes and tucked them round Webster. Then she came back upstairs to tuck in Tom.

"It wouldn't be fair to warm up Webster," she said gently. "He might wake up by your radiator, but then he wouldn't be able to cope outdoors. He needs to wake up naturally."

Christmas Eve came and Tom hung up his stocking. At the last moment he scribbled a note and left it at the end of his bed.

Tom woke up long before it was light.

"Better not wake Mum yet," he muttered. He felt for his torch.

"OOOOH!" His stocking was full to bursting. Tom was itching to look inside. But first he wanted to check on Webster... just in case.

Tom crept down to the garage. For a moment he thought he could hear rustling noises. He crossed his fingers and shone his torch. Two startled eyes looked back at him!

"WOW!" cried Tom. He moved his torch beam and it played on a smart new cage, right by Webster's box. On top of the cage was a note and some tinsel.

Suddenly the garage flooded with light.

"MERRY CHRISTMAS!" cried Mum. She danced up and down and hugged Tom.

Tom hugged Mum back. Then he looked serious.

"SSSHHH!" hissed Tom loudly. "We don't want to wake Webster, do we?"

Christmas is coming,
The geese are getting fat,
Please to put a penny
In the old man's hat.
If you haven't got a penny,
A ha'penny will do;
If you haven't got a ha'penny,
Then God bless you!

Christmas Food

An important part of Christmas celebrations is the preparation of special Christmas food.

In medieval times, huge feasts were served in the homes of rich noblemen at Christmas. The feasts often began with a boar's head, decorated with herbs, holly and an apple, and this was followed by pheasant, swan, peacock and capon.

For ordinary people, a goose was the traditional Christmas bird, and in many European countries it is still the most popular. Turkeys were brought over from America in the sixteenth century and have since replaced the goose as the main dish at Christmas in many homes.

In England, mince pies are a Christmas favourite. The first mince pies were filled with finely chopped or minced mutton. Later, raisins, currants, eggs, sugar and spices were added. Today, meat is no longer used in mince pies, although suet, which is animal fat, is a common ingredient.

The traditional day for making Christmas puddings is 'stir-up Sunday' at the beginning of advent. The ingredients — currants, raisins, sultanas, suet, breadcrumbs, eggs and spices — must always be stirred from East to West in honour of the three Wise Men. Every member of the family must stir the pudding and make a secret wish.

Jingle Bells

Dashing through the snow
In a one-horse open sleigh,
O'er the fields we go,
Laughing all the way.
Bells on bob-tail ring,
Making spirits bright.
What fun it is to ride and sing
A sleighing song tonight.

Jingle bells, jingle bells,
Jingle all the way.
Oh, what fun it is to ride
In a one-horse open sleigh.
Jingle bells, jingle bells,
Jingle all the way.
Oh, what fun it is to ride
In a one-horse open sleigh.

Now the ground is white
Go it while you're young.
Take the girls tonight,
Sing this sleighing song.
Get a bob-tailed bay,
Two-forty for his speed.
Then hitch him to an open sleigh
And you will take the lead.

Three Presents for the Prince

There once was a prince called Vincent. His family had fallen on hard times, so they sold up their magnificent palace and moved to 43b Magnolia Road.

Now Vincent had three sisters – Vanessa, Veronica and Victoria. There was no room for servants at 43b, nor indeed could the family afford them. But Vincent was lazy and made servants of his sisters.

All day long, Vincent's voice could be heard the length and breadth of Magnolia Road.

"Vanessa, I need a new button on my shirt."

"Veronica, turn on the television. It's time for my favourite programme."

"UGH! Victoria, there's no sugar in my hot chocolate."

As time went by the princesses grew thinner and more weary. Vincent grew fatter and more lazy. Although he had a room all to himself, you couldn't move in it. The floor was strewn with sweet wrappers and rubbish. The bed was covered in comics and chaos.

The princesses were already beginning to dread Christmas.

"Vincent will want an enormous present," sighed Vanessa.

"He'll expect a mammoth meal," groaned Veronica.

"And WE'LL have to entertain him all day long," said Victoria.

Sure enough, as soon as December came, Vincent started.

"Vanessa, I want a really SPECIAL present this year.

"Veronica, make sure you make the biggest Christmas pudding ever.

"And Victoria, don't forget to arrange some party games. I can't be expected to amuse myself."

The sisters decided that they could stand it no longer. They had to do something about Vincent.

That evening Vanessa, Veronica and Victoria huddled together in their bedroom to plot and scheme. Every now and then they giggled.

"Hey! What's going on?" cried Vincent. It was a long time since he'd heard his sisters laugh.

"We're just planning Christmas," they shouted back.

"Good!" cried Vincent. He snuggled down under the comics and chaos and was soon asleep.

On Christmas morning four stockings hung by the fireplace.

"But mine's only the same size as yours," grumbled Vincent. "And *my* Christmas list was *much* longer."

Vanessa, Veronica and Victoria unpacked their stockings and admired their gifts. Vincent tore open his parcels and stuffed the paper down the side of the settee.

"Hurry up, girls!" he cried. "I want to open the presents you've bought me next. I bought you some sweets, but I've eaten them all."

Vincent went over to the tree. There were three large presents. Each was beautifully wrapped and had a matching label.

Vincent grabbed the nearest parcel.

"Don't forget to read the label," said Vanessa.

But Vincent couldn't wait. Off came the paper and out came the present. Vincent's face fell.

"What is it?" he cried.

"It's a toy box," said Vanessa, "an empty toy box."

Then Vincent read the label.

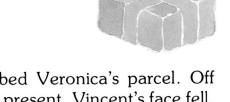

> "I looked for a space
> To put a new toy,
> But Vince, you're such
> An untidy boy
> That before I give you
> Anything more,
> You'll have to clear
> A space on your floor!"

Vincent turned pink and grabbed Veronica's parcel. Off came the paper and out came the present. Vincent's face fell. "What are all these?" he cried.

"They're ingredients," said Veronica, "lots of them."

Then Vincent read the label.

> "If you want a pudding,
> You lover of food,
> You must be polite
> Instead of rude.
> And before you eat
> This Christmas Day,
> You'll have to heed
> What your sisters say!"

Vincent turned red and grabbed Victoria's parcel. Off came the paper and out came the present. Vincent's face fell. "What are they?" he cried.

"They're a dustpan and brush," said Victoria. "And some dustbin liners."

Then Vincent read the label.

"Just listen to me
If Vince is your name,
While I explain
The name of the game.
It's called *Tidy Up*
And *Sort out the Mess*
And *Save up to Buy
Your Sisters a Dress*."

Vincent turned purple and shot upstairs. There was a lot of banging about and then it went quiet. At last Vincent came downstairs again. He took a deep breath.

"If I tidy up my room and help with the chores and learn how to sew on buttons and how to give presents as well as receive them, will you show me how to make a Christmas pudding?"

"Yes!" said Vanessa. "Yes!" said Veronica. "Yes!" said Victoria. And anyone in Magnolia Road will tell you that the prince and princesses lived happily ever after.

The Twelve Days of Christmas

On the first day of Christmas
my true love sent to me,
a partridge in a pear tree.

On the second day of Christmas
my true love sent to me,
two turtledoves
and a partridge in a pear tree.

On the third day of Christmas
my true love sent to me,
three French hens,
two turtledoves
and a partridge in a pear tree.

On the fourth day of Christmas
my true love sent to me,
four calling birds...

On the fifth day of Christmas
my true love sent to me,
five gold rings...

On the sixth day of Christmas
my true love sent to me,
six geese a-laying...

On the seventh day of Christmas
my true love sent to me,
seven swans a-swimming...

On the eighth day of Christmas
my true love sent to me,
eight maids a-milking...